RAINY DAY MAGIC

MARIE-LOUISE GAY

Stoddart

A PANDA PICTURE BOOK

Published in 1992 by
Stoddart Publishing Co. Limited
34 Lesmill Road
Toronto, Canada
M3B 2T6

Published in hardcover and quality paperback in 1987 by
Stoddart Publishing Co. Limited

Canadian Cataloguing in Publication Data

Gay, Marie-Louise
    Rainy day magic

"Panda picture books".
ISBN 0-7736-7366-0

I. Title

PS8563.A8R3 1992   jC813'.54   C92-093289-4
PZ7.G3Ra 1992

Printed in Canada

It's rainy and foggy
And boring and gray.
"Hey Daddy, there's Joey.
She's coming to play!"

My dad had a headache.
He said, "*Please*, no noise."

So ever so softly
We cruised through my toys.

We raced down the hallway
And round past the door,

Up over the couch and then
– CRASH – to the floor.

My dad got so angry.
We barreled downstairs,
And built a great castle
From creaky old chairs.

Then a flash! and a bang!
It was darker than night,
Except in the corner –
A little blue light.

"Hey Victor. What *is* that?"
Said Joey, "Let's see."
And Joey went first
'Cause she's braver than me.

The blue turned to purple
Then black and then gray.

We crawled to a place
Where banana trees sway.

"What weird grass," said Joey.
"It's yellow and black.

Hey, this isn't grass.
It's a bumblebee's back!"

"BUMBLEBEE???!!!" roared Tiger.
(I'm sure he woke Dad.)

"Sorry," cried Joey.
"Oh, please don't get mad."

"ATCHOO," sneezed the tiger
We both tumbled down.

A slippery slide
On a snake's scaly gown.

"Hang on," hissed the snake.
"Come slither wis-s-s-s-s-s-s me."

But Joey fell off
And splashed into the sea.

So I dived in after
And – brrr – was it cold!

We swam through a swirl
Of blue, green, and gold.

A sea-horse was winning
At sea-solitaire.
A tiny mauve starfish said,

"Hello there."

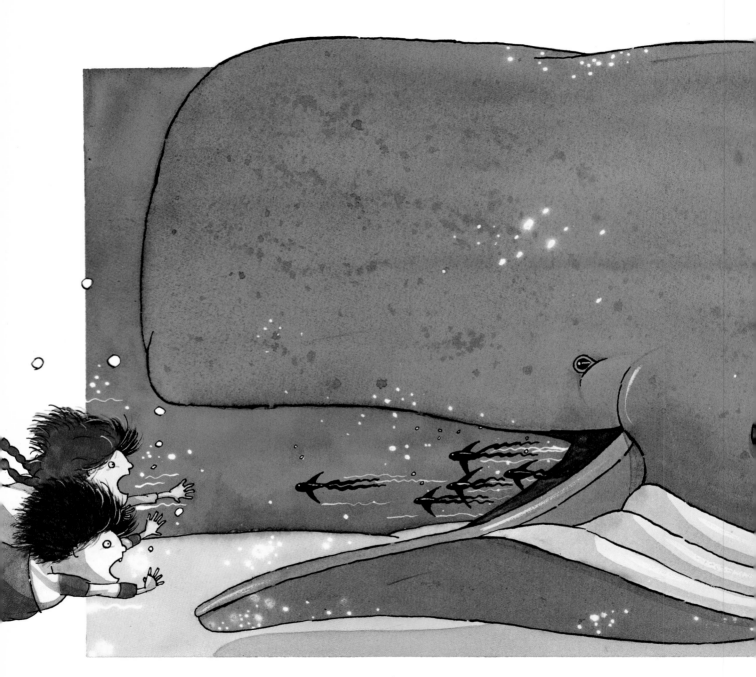

"HEY KIDS," boomed a whale.
"YA GOIN' MY WAY?

YA DON'T NEED A TICKET.
SO WHADDYA SAY?"

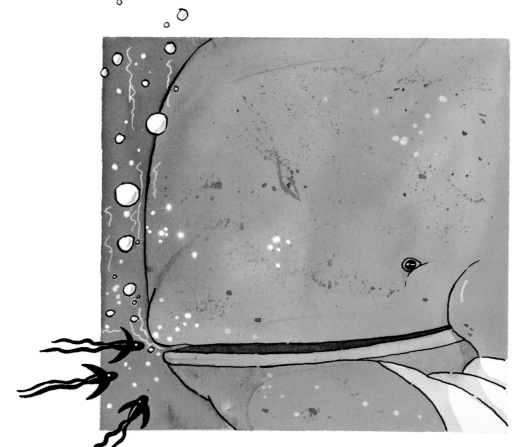

"No thanks," replied Joey.
And what a mistake.
He swallowed us up
Like two pieces of cake.

The dark was so scary.
Now what would we do?
"Oh, Victor," said Joey.
"What's that? Is that you?"

And – "Supper!" called Mom,
As she opened the door.

And light flooded down
To the basement's dark floor.

I tried not to giggle,
I tried not to stare
When Daddy said, "Joey!
What's that in your hair?!"